P9-ASG-528

READ TO ACHIEVE
c/o Parents' Choice Foundation
Box 185, Newton, Massachusetts 02168

TO THE CHILDREN OF

NEW HAVEN PUBLIC LIBRARIES

FROM ALL YOUR FRIENDS AT

PRINCESS HOUSE, INC.

For Marian

Copyright text and illustrations © 1991 Amanda Loverseed
First published 1991 by Blackie and Son Ltd

A CIP catalogue record for the book is available from the British
Library.

ISBN 0-216-93064-2

Blackie and Son Ltd
7 Leicester Place
London WC2H 7BP

First American edition published in 1991 by
Peter Bedrick Books
2112 Broadway
New York, NY 10023

Library of Congress Cataloging-in-Publication Data
Loverseed, Amanda.
Thunder King: a Peruvian folk tale/Amanda Loverseed.
--1st American ed.
Summary: The great bird Condor helps Illanti rescue his twin
brother from King Thunder's ice palace high in the mountains.
ISBN 87226-450-5
[1. Folklore--Peru.] I. Title.
PZ8.1.L948Th   1991
398.24'528912--dc20
[E]   90-14416   CIP   AC

Printed in Hong Kong by Wing King Tong Co. Ltd.

A Peruvian Folk Tale

THE THUNDER KING

Folk Tales of the World

AMANDA LOVERSEED

Blackie
London

Bedrick/Blackie
New York

Tantay and Illanti had been born within minutes of one another in their parents' little round house high in the windswept plains of Peru. These special brothers loved each other dearly and could not bear to be separated. Only their mother could tell the twins apart.

Their home had clay walls, a mossy roof and two windows which looked out on the maize and potato fields, the llamas on the hills and the high snow-covered mountains.

Usually the brothers worked together but one day their
mother gave them separate jobs.

'Illanti, today you must go into the hills and look after
the llamas. Tantay, you go to the fields and scare the
birds away from the crops.'

Sad to spend the day apart, they said goodbye. Tantay
waved as his brother set off for the hills.

Tantay worked very hard running about to keep the birds away from the crops. He thought of Illanti high in the hills. Suddenly he noticed that it was getting very dark. Looking into the sky he saw storm clouds gathering.

'That looks like a thunder storm,' thought Tantay. He was right. High up over the horizon flew Thunder, King of the Skies. Thunder roared and raged across the country with his winds and clouds, looking for things to steal. Sometimes he stole food, sometimes he stole people.

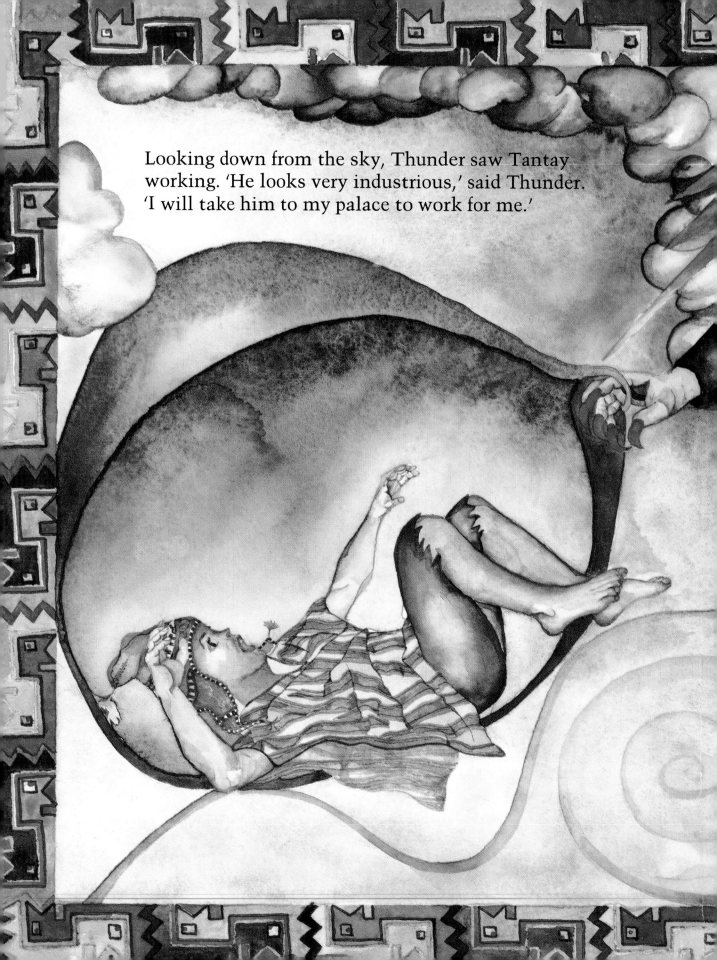

Looking down from the sky, Thunder saw Tantay working. 'He looks very industrious,' said Thunder. 'I will take him to my palace to work for me.'

Tantay watched the storm come closer.

'I must go inside,' he thought. 'I hope Illanti will be safe on the hills.' As he turned towards the house, Thunder sent a powerful gust of wind that lifted Tantay off his feet. Thunder swept down from the skies catching Tantay in a sack. Pulling tight the string, he carried the terrified boy away into the storm.

Meanwhile, Illanti had been looking after the llamas. As he watched the animals grazing he too noticed the clouds gathering, turning the sky black and stormy. A sudden fear for his brother made Illanti turn towards the field where Tantay had been working. At that very moment he saw with horror Thunder capturing Tantay.

'Whatever can I do?' cried Illanti. Suddenly a llama stepped forward. Its large brown eyes were kind and full of pity. It spoke.

'Thunder will take Tantay to his palace. I will show

you part of the way. It is a dangerous journey.' The other llamas nodded in agreement.

'I am not afraid,' said Illanti bravely. 'Please show me the way.' Together they turned to face the distant mountains.

After a long walk they reached a deep gorge with a fast-running river at the bottom. The llama stopped.

'I cannot cross the river. You must go on alone into the mountains. Look for Condor, the most beautiful bird in the world. He will help you.'

Illanti waved as the llama turned to go home.

Around the corner was a circular, stone house with a very fat smiling woman sitting outside stripping corn cobs into a basket. An even fatter man appeared at the door.

'Do you want to cross the gorge?' he called. Illanti said that he did.

'Sit in this basket. I will pull you over on the rope to the other side. Just hold tight.'

Illanti felt frightened as the basket crossed the gorge. He closed his eyes but very soon reached the other side. Stepping with relief out of the basket, Illanti waved his thanks.

Illanti walked all day. Soon the ground became very steep and the air colder. Illanti looked into the sky and there, flying directly above him, was the most beautiful bird he had ever seen. He knew this was Condor. Reaching for his panpipes, Illanti played a low and sorrowful tune. The notes floated upwards to the Condor circling in the setting sun. He glided gracefully to land at Illanti's feet.

'Little one,' said Condor, 'you have called me from the skies, but your tune is one of sadness. What is wrong?'

'Oh, Condor, Thunder stole my twin
brother. I wonder if you could help me find
Thunder's palace and save Tantay.'

'Thunder lives at the very top of this
mountain. His palace is surrounded by rock
and ice and very few people escape. I will
help you, but it will be dangerous. As you
have no wings, I will lend you mine.
Climb on to my back.'

Illanti clung to Condor as they
journeyed upwards.

At last, Illanti and Condor reached the palace. The walls
rose high out of the rocks. The windows were made of
ice.

'We will never save Tantay,' cried Illanti in
desperation.

Suddenly the sky started to darken, concealing them in
shadows. Soon, Thunder's winds came flying around the
palace.

'Thunder must be preparing to leave the palace for the
night. We may have a chance to free Tantay,' whispered
Condor,

The large palace doors opened and there stood Thunder
in all his terrifying glory. The doors closed behind him.
With a mighty cry from Thunder the winds gathered
around him and they all flew into the sky.

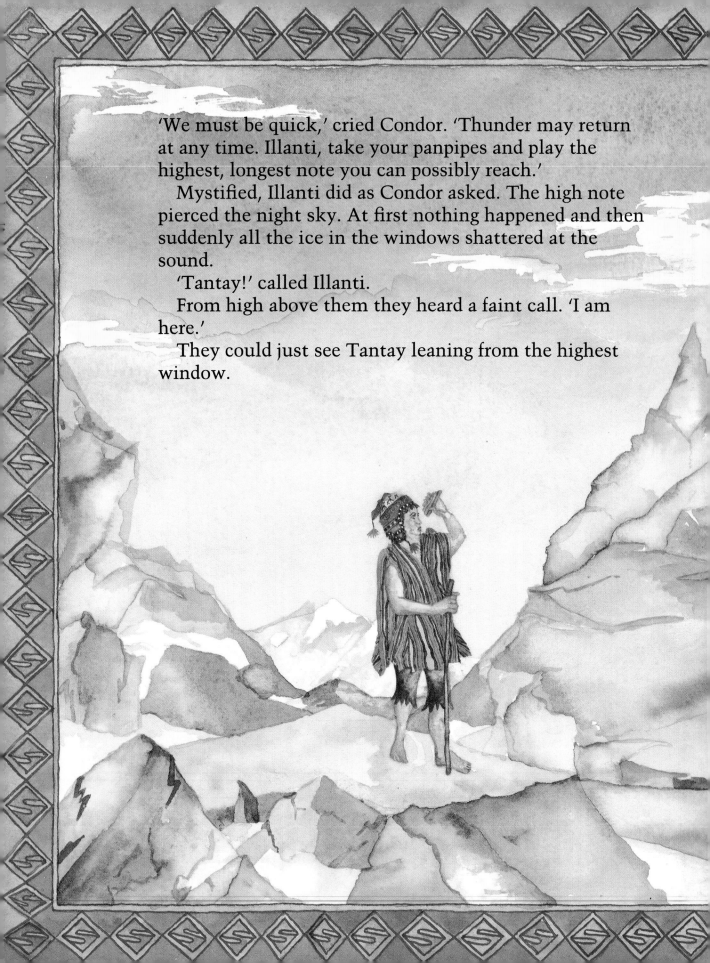

'We must be quick,' cried Condor. 'Thunder may return at any time. Illanti, take your panpipes and play the highest, longest note you can possibly reach.'

Mystified, Illanti did as Condor asked. The high note pierced the night sky. At first nothing happened and then suddenly all the ice in the windows shattered at the sound.

'Tantay!' called Illanti.

From high above them they heard a faint call. 'I am here.'

They could just see Tantay leaning from the highest window.

Illanti climbed on to
Condor's back and they flew
up to the window. Condor
hovered as near as possible while
Illanti helped Tantay from the window
on to Condor's back.

'I knew you would rescue me,' cried Tantay as the two
brothers hugged one another. Condor rose in the air.
They could hear Thunder rumbling in the distance.

'We must be out of sight before Thunder
returns,' called Condor. 'Do not worry.
Thunder will not follow us. By the time he
returns, the windows will have iced over again
and he will not even realise Tantay has escaped.'

The two brothers embraced each other as Condor flew them home over the mountains and hills. Illanti pointed out the little round house by the bridge. They both waved at the llamas. At last their home was in sight.

Condor landed in the field where Tantay had been
working. Illanti and Tantay thanked Condor very much
for all his help. They watched together as the beautiful
bird circled overhead and flew back towards the
mountains.

As Tantay and Illanti entered the house their mother was stirring a pot on the stove.

'Just in time for supper,' she said. 'Did you manage to keep the birds out of the field, Tantay?' The brothers looked at one another and laughed.

'Nearly all the birds,' said Tantay, as he thought of Condor. The brothers sat together by the fire. They felt sleepy after all their adventures but they were happy because they were together again.